THICKER THAN WATER

By

Michael McDonnell

1

Kenmare Abbey:

It was an odd place for a cemetery, right in the middle of the old abbey ruins overlooking the bay. Gravestones were strewn through the nave and chancel, giving the impression that the tombs had been there first and the ancient walls built around them. 'Gone to God. September 14th 1754,' next to 'May his soul rest in peace, 20th March 1998,' testified to the span of time since the people of this part of Ireland first decided land was of more value to the living than the dead and kept their burials within the walls of the abbey. A tall, lone figure stooped in front of an old stone that lay flat just inside a small ante-room. He looked like a mourner come to pay his respects to the dead. Through the decades of growth of lichen and moss, it was still just possible to see the words, 'Anthony Shaughnessy. Died 1857.' His head bowed, he stood silent in a silent landscape, examining the grave closely as if to make sure of the identity of its occupant. Then he spat out the word, 'bastard,' turned and walked to his car.

Kenmare:

Dermot O'Hara awoke. He opened his eyes and could only see the vague outline of the window in the darkness. O'Hara sighed, turned and checked the time. 3.18. He'd been dreaming that he'd landed the biggest cod ever caught in West Cork and was standing alongside the massive fish, accepting the plaudits of dignitaries from far and wide. If St. Peter was a fisherman then Dermot was a super-fisherman. But where Peter had been a fisher of souls, Dermot was a fisher of sinners, or a policeman as the more prosaic would have it. Mind you, he often wondered how essential it was to have an upholder of law that was rarely broken in the small town of Kenmare. What was his last case? Ah yes, the interesting affair of Mrs McGann and her missing library ticket. That would have troubled Holmes no doubt but he'd solved it in seconds. It was in her handbag. O'Hara wasn't too bothered about the lack of crime though, happy enough with a state of affairs where police duty rarely impinged on his real love, the pursuit of the many species of fish that thronged the waters around this part of the coast. Still, all his investigative instincts were alert now, for something had woken him up. Above the soft breathing of his wife Joanne, he could hear an unfamiliar sound somewhere in the house. During the Spring and Summer they offered two rooms to guests, a small business which Joanne had started during the

4

school holidays from the local primary where she taught Maths. Now they had one visitor, an American by the name of McMahon. An intelligent, affable man, McMahon nevertheless aroused the suspicion of the policeman in O'Hara. Unlike most American tourists they entertained, he showed no interest in Kenmare or its people. Normally Dermot or Joanne would answer at length questions about their visitors' namesakes but McMahon not only didn't ask but already seemed very well versed in local goings on.

'He's up and about again,' Dermot whispered to Joanne who ignored him. 'I said he's...'

'I heard you!' Joanne growled through gritted teeth. 'So what? I'm trying to sleep. Do you want us to have a curfew on our guests? Maybe he's a vampire.'

Dermot considered this for a moment and smiled. The stout, red faced American would make an unlikely vampire. But certainly he had odd habits.

'Have you noticed the scars on his cheek and neck?'

'Yes I have.' Joanne muttered tersely. Now go to sleep!'

'Sorry. Alright. Where do you think he got them?

She sighed, 'He's old enough to have seen action in Vietnam.

'That's what I thought.

'So why are you asking me? Will you just go to sleep!

The front door closed gently. 3.22 in the morning was a strange time to go

out for a walk. Dermot pondered this for the few seconds it took him to fall

asleep and start dreaming that his old enemy, Assistant Commissioner

Quinn, had just been eaten by a shark.

The guesthouse breakfast room faced east, looking out from the hillside over

the sparkling waters of the inlet. Walking in next morning with the day's

post in hand, O'Hara was surprised to see that McMahon was ignoring the

stunning view and reading a usually tedious local paper. The American

greeted his host ebulliently, 'Morning Dermot, have you seen this thing here

about the drop in your fishing stocks. I'm surprised you fishermen ever

catch anything with these foreign trawlers hoovering up fish by the ton.'

This was a favourite hobby horse of Dermot's. He and his brother, a

trawlerman, had fallen out over it and hadn't spoken for six months. Joanne

came in and shot him a glance that silenced him before he could get going.

Looking over at their visitor she smiled and asked, 'So how's Count Dracula

this morning?'

McMahon looked up from the paper startled.

'Morning Joanne! Huh, so you heard me sneak out last night. Sorry if I

disturbed you. You know what it is? I find it hard to sleep here – it's too quiet. Now in NY we'd be out catching bad guys at that time – I walk out at three a.m. here and what is there? Nothing!! Silence! Can't hear a siren or a gunshot. Not even the neighbours yelling and rowing! I tell you it's unnatural.'

Still grinning he turned to Dermot.

'Seriously, it always takes me a week or so to adjust to how quiet Ireland is.'

'Long may it stay that way,' muttered the Garda from behind the sports section of the paper, the only part which he read.

'That's your problem Dermot, you can only catch fish. Now if they've been misbehaving that's fine but it's not the same as a good criminal. When was your last murder?'

Joanne looked with some alarm at the American as she returned carrying a plate containing enough cholesterol to kill a precinct full of cops.

'Full Irish breakfast as usual Frank?'

'That looks just great Joanne.'

The phone rang and Dermot pulled a face. He'd been eager to resume his chat about fishing and homicide but the delight would have to wait. Less important business called. Joanne could hear his voice in the hallway.

'Sean, how you doing? What? Really? That's all I needed. I'm supposed to be fishing today. Where was he last seen? Up by the waterfall? Yeah, yeah, I

7

know where you mean, the old village nearer the road. Well if he hasn't broken anything yet, I'll break something for him when I get there. OK. I'll be as quick as I can.' He stormed back into the breakfast room.

'Isn't that just typical! That was Sean. He's at the station. I'm afraid Frank, Denis Grogan at the Ardmoy Hotel has reported one of your fellow countrymen missing - seems to have got himself lost on the mountain up at Coomnakilla. Last year we had to helicopter a Dutch guy off there after he broke an ankle – took six hours to find him and get him to hospital. Ah well, at least last night was warm he should be OK. Jo, if Peter calls can you let him know I'm going to be late getting to the boat today. And tell him to get a mobile will you, he's impossible to contact. His excuse is that the radio waves of mobile phones frighten the fish – bloody nonsense! Excuse my French. Tell him I'll see him in Crowley's around eight or so if I don't get down to the boat in time. Anyway I'd better go and get this eejit off the mountain in one piece.'

They heard him slam the front door, start his car and deposit most of the gravel on the driveway against the wall as he accelerated away. Joanne raised her eyebrows at Frank and looked to Heaven.

'God give me patience – he'll be in a temper now for days. If his fishing's disrupted that's it. I sometimes think it's the only thing he thinks about. He was offered a promotion and a salary rise you know – we'd have been located to Mullingar; but of course that's inland so he turned it down.' She paused and looked out of the window, the peaceful view as ever restoring some degree of calm. 'You don't have any obsessions like that do you?' 'Oh I dare say my wife could have listed a few but none I can think of. Mind you I guess you don't know your own faults until you're really tested.' He broke off and stared intently at his empty plate.

The road to Coomnakilla took Dermot across the new bridge and up a long rough track. Gaggles of hikers straggled along the road, red-faced in the unseasonal heat. Turning off the track, a bumpy, steep, grassy lane led onto the mountainside then gave way to scrub and bracken leaving drivers to steer by local knowledge. That knowledge had to be good. All around were peat bogs that could swallow a walker or even a four wheel drive vehicle. Dermot noticed a small group ahead on the right, just a few yards from the empty shell of an old farmhouse. Looking at the place O'Hara imagined the family driven by starvation from these strong walls and the beauty of this setting to the squalid, overcrowded brownstone tenements of New York. They hadn't even run to a better life, just a better chance of survival. One of the group was the head of the local mountain rescue. 'Some bloody Yank with a broken leg again?' Dermot asked tetchily, looking beyond the mountainside to the diamond blue sea where he should have been in an hour. 'I'm afraid it's a bit more serious this time Dermot. He's dead. We found him quickly enough just over an hour ago. I'd guess it was a coronary, it's a steep old climb and he's not exactly the fittest looking character I've ever seen.'

' Jeez!' hissed Dermot, I'll give Andy McAteer a call.'

'We called him – he's over there talking to the paramedics.'

'Efficient as ever! Right, where is the poor bastard?'

As O'Hara said this, he saw the local GP, McAteer, a few yards ahead. The tall bearded figure unbent from where he had been examining the body and greeted the policeman. Dermot went up to him and saw the unfortunate American. He lay face down, one arm by his side, one forward as if to protect himself from a fall.

O'Hara looked at the doctor expectantly;

'Any clues as to what happened Andy?'

'Probably his heart. Cigarettes, beer, burgers and golf; a deadly combination.

'When do you reckon he died?'

'That's an interesting one Dermot. He's been dead for some time. I would reckon, maybe a day or so.'

'Strange no one found him until now?'

'Ay, though he's hidden behind that hill – walkers tend to skirt around it on the other side.'

'I was just wondering that; what's he doing over here, away from the path I mean?'

That, I suppose, is for you to find out. Right, can't hang about here all day, let's get him into the Land Rover and off to the fridge. He'll have to go to Killarney for autopsy. Do you want to come along Dermot? I know there's nothing you like better than a good carve up.'

McAteer never seemed to take life too seriously, once causing a scare in the town by telling an elderly, gullible farmer that his mild cold might be the beginning of bubonic plague. Dermot declined the offer.

'I'd better find out where he's from and contact his relatives. I might be able to use our tame American who's staying with us for some help with that. Peaceful spot to go I suppose,' the policeman mused to the rescue team as they put the body on a stretcher. They looked at the view, so familiar to them it always seemed slightly odd that people would travel halfway round the world to visit.

Rory Duncan, the team leader grimaced slightly, 'Aye. Maybe so. I doubt if he would have enjoyed it that much though.'

'You don't think he could have fallen?'

'Where from Dermot? This part of the hills isn't too steep and he's got no injuries that I can see.'

'Ah well, looks pretty straightforward, I can get an afternoon out in the boat then.'

They picked the victim up gently, carried him over and laid him in the back of the mountain rescue Land Rover. O' Hara followed, with the doctor behind him. He'd write a quick report and get off down to the jetty where Foley's boat was moored. It was now just after eleven. Hopefully he could get there in time to catch Foley. Just to make sure no one would get in his way he turned on the siren and lights as he pulled out onto the main road and headed for town.

The Lough:

Peter Foley stood on the broad afterdeck of his fishing boat watching the police car's blue flashing light coming along the coast road and smiled to himself. Usually the only time siren and lights were used was when Gardai Dermot O'Hara was late for a fishing trip. The car avoided the bollards on the pier and slid to a halt inches from the edge. Foley clambered up from the deck where he'd been preparing to untie and push away from the quayside. 'Twenty seconds later and I'd have been gone Dermot, what's kept you?' Opening the boot O'Hara was lifting out three fishing rods, a plastic box of bait and an assortment of hooks. He looked up at Foley and not for the first time, felt he was looking at a throwback to the Vikings who had settled these parts a thousand years before. The fisherman was six feet two with a shaggy mane of fair hair and an unkempt beard. The policeman grunted as he lifted the tackle onto the boat, 'American tourist died of heart failure on Coomnakilla. Had to get him picked up by the Mountain Rescue lads.' He followed Foley down a rusting ladder on to the foredeck. They cast off and headed round the end of the small concrete pier protecting the harbour from the vicious winds of winter that poured down the glen like javelins. It was a warm, clear day and Dermot felt at home as he luxuriated in the breeze mixed with the smell of fish and diesel that permeated Foley's boat. The

13

inlet was narrow and he could clearly hear the noise of the children in the playground of the primary school. Every rock on the shore brought back one memory or another; here the tall angled black granite reminded him of the fear they had experienced on a bitter November night when, after losing an engine and all power, they had struggled into harbour guided only by the lights of cars on land,. He saw the field running down to the little beach where they had landed to rescue an injured seal on a hot July day ten or more years ago. Looking down at his hand, he could still see the neat white scar where the seal had repaid their kindness with a sharp nip and remembered Foley's amusement.

'Think of them like dogs Dermot, but in this case their bite *is* worse than their bark.'

A loud voice disturbed him from his reverie.

'Hey Dermot you can cast now, we're out of the sterile zone.'

'What's that?'

'If you take a line from Reen Point to Timanoe there are very few fish between there and the harbour.'

'Why do you think that is?' asked Dermot.

'You'd hardly see a seal either until you get past the line.'

Dermot knew he was about to get the whole 'Brussels bureaucrats have destroyed the fish stocks,' speech, so he decided to launch a pre-emptive query.

'Why don't the fish come further in than that?'

'And why don't you stop asking me and take a couple of mackerel down to the station for questioning.' Foley was grinning from ear to ear. Eccentric he might be but there were few who knew the sea's tides and the behaviour of its inhabitants as well as this guy.

'Hey Dermot, mentioning mackerel, did I tell you about Martin the mackerel?' O'Hara looked warily at him.

'Go on then.'

'There was a mackerel run last week while I was out with a boatload of Yanks and Germans. You know the way mackerel are so dim they'll jump into your hand when they're in that sort of mood. Well I told them that I'd spent years taming one mackerel after finding him abandoned, leant over the side and picked one up. Told them his name was Martin and he followed the boat wherever I went. They believed me.' Foley roared with laughter. 'A friendly enough lot though.' He paused. 'Except for one guy who didn't appreciate my charms at all. But I forgave him when I saw his scars.'

'What scars?' said Dermot, suddenly alert.

'I'm no doctor but I'd say they were bullet wounds.'

'Sounds like McMahon! He's our guest at the moment. Big guy, white hair?
Were the scars on his cheek and neck? '

'Ay. That must be him. Weird guy if you ask me.'

'Why do you say that?'

'Here we go questions, questions.'

'No seriously.'

'Well, for a start he took no interest in the seals. OK not everyone comes
out just for them but normally people take at least a bit of a look. Not a bit of
it. He had his binoculars pointed at the mountain all the time.'

'Can you remember which part?'

'I'll point it out when we get there.' He stopped and looked at Dermot.
'Now I think about it funnily enough - it was just opposite Coomnakilla. I
didn't take much notice of him once I realised he wasn't taking in my hugely
witty and entertaining repartee.'

O'Hara stared at him for a minute.

'That's an odd coincidence that he should be scanning the hill up there, just
where this guy was found this morning.'

'That's just what I was thinking,' said Foley, 'but of course he may have
been looking at other parts and I didn't notice him…maybe.'

'But you don't believe that.'

'No not really. With all the health and safety nonsense I have to put up with when carrying the public, I keep an eye on all of them and after Coomnakilla he didn't seem to look at much else. Anyway we're here to fish not catch murderers!.'

Foley went to the bow and let down a sea anchor. They put the rods together then Foley took the port side, O'Hara the starboard and they settled down. As if in meditation, they each let the peace of the inlet and their concentration blank out the outside world. Dermot looked over the side into the grey green depths and the oily lift and drop of the water lulled him so that all that existed in the world was the patch of water where his line disappeared into the depths. Yet every so often, his focus would be broken by thoughts of the two Americans who had entered his life in the last week. Instinctively he felt they were linked, an invisible strand joining them and him, drawing them closer to each other. 'Leave well alone and don't go prying into something that could cause disruption and trouble,' he told himself. Suddenly he heard Foley shout, 'What the hell is this.' His rod was bent over 90 degrees and the tip was close to the surface of the sea while the reel whirred as line was pulled at high speed. Whatever was on the other end was big and in no mood to give in. Twenty minutes later by the time they had both struggled with and eventually landed a four and a half foot conger eel, Dermot had completely forgotten all Americans and could not have cared less. His dream of the previous night had almost come true. He told Foley about this.

'It always worries me when policemen start developing psychic powers Dermot,' joked the big fisherman. 'That fella's taken it out of me - I could do with a pint. When we get in I'll have to clean up the boat for tomorrow's trip - a load of school kids are doing a study of the seals in the bay. Once I'm done I'll see you in Crowley's.' Dermot looked at the conger reluctantly. 'I suppose we'd best head back. I've got forms to fill in, as always.' Foley started the engine and they pushed the boat's bow across the current, turning towards the vague smudge of the town some three miles away over the water.

Assistant Commissioner Quinn:

As they rounded the end of the pier and even before they moored, Dermot

knew he had a problem. Through Foley's binoculars, he could see Jo on the

quayside, looking like thunder.

'Dermot, where's your mobile?' O'Hara knew he'd left it in his car, a

deliberate act to ensure he wasn't disturbed from his fishing.

'I must have left it somewhere,' he said sheepishly remembering his

complaint about Foley not having a phone. His wife stared at him,

exasperated.

'Headquarters in Killarney have been trying to get you for the last two

hours. Assistant Commissioner Quinn's been on. I don't know what you've

been doing but you'd better get on to him now.'

Dermot looked at Peter. 'This sounds a bit more serious than a few forms…

See you later Peter. Let's make it Crowley's at 8.00?'

'Fine, that's if you haven't been hung drawn and quartered by then of

course!'

The Garda station, a substantial building that might have been mistaken for a

hotel, was in the centre of Kenmare, just off the main square. Dermot's car

came to a halt outside it and he sprinted up the six steps, through the front door and executed a sharp left into his office. He just stopped himself

knocking the Assistant Commissioner for the West of Ireland across his

desk.

Assistant Commissioner Quinn, a gaunt, saturnine figure some 6 feet 4 in

height, seemed to grow an extra foot. 'Good afternoon Garda O'Hara. How

was the fishing?' he said in a voice dripping with disapproval.

'Fine, sir, very good indeed. Managed to catch a conger eel.'

'Really? I hope you're as good at catching a murderer.'

'What?' Dermot wasn't sure he'd heard right. Looking to the side, he saw

Andy McAteer. O'Hara had never seen the doctor look as serious as he did

now. McAteer stepped forward.

'Our American tourist, Dermot. When they got him to Killarney they took a

blood sample which indicated he'd been subjected to an overdose of a heart

drug – he may have been killed somewhere else and dumped at

Coomnakilla.'

'And unfortunately he's not just an ordinary tourist the AC added. 'He is or

was Senator Mark Shaughnessy, a senator for Iowa. A prominent Democrat,

in the American sense, but also a Vietnam veteran with a string of

decorations. The US Ambassador has already been on asking what I'm

doing to catch his killer.' O'Hara looked from the doctor to his commanding officer and suddenly felt deeply inadequate. Thinking of his

two assistant constables, he knew that the three of them were not used to this

level of investigation.

'OK Andy let's get back up to Coomnakilla. I need a dozen men sir to

search the area for clues. Can you authorise that immediately sir?'

'It's already done O'Hara. You have full access to any resource you need

but don't go telling too many people that - it's, well, politically a bit difficult

at the minute shall we say.' The AC looked uncomfortably at both men.

'We're planning to close a number of stations this year and rationalise them

into regional centres.' Dermot could imagine which sort of stations were for

the chop. Looking around the room and across a corridor to another side

room the AC commented.

'This is a fine big building O'Hara. It's all for you and your two assistants?'

'That's right sir, we hold crime surgeries in the room across the way.' He

thought back to the last one six months ago. One farmer had turned up to

ask if the Gardai could help him with a boundary dispute. Since then the

room had lain empty and he prayed that the AC wouldn't go in or venture

upstairs and see the five vacant rooms there.

'Well O'Hara, I trust you can sort this out as soon as possible without too

much outside help and give me a good reason to keep this expensive piece of real estate for our use.' said the AC, glancing up at the elegant ivy covered front as he left the station.

'Good luck and call my office if you need anything.'

When Dermot got back inside McAteer was spreading a map across the table and glanced at him, 'If you solve this you'll be flavour of the month and no mistake.'

'A big "if" Andy. I mean how many murders have you known in this town over the last twenty, thirty, in fact you could probably go back a hundred years and not come across anything? Then one comes along and it's a real whopper, a bloody American politician war hero. So, no pressure to solve it eh? And if I don't, well, your man could see how valuable this building is. Just when the government wants us to cut back.'

He sighed and turned back to the task in hand.

The two men leant over the map for several minutes working out how far a body could feasibly be carried. They had created a circle, the centre of which was the site where the corpse was found.

'This doesn't help much does it?' mused the policeman. 'He could have been killed anywhere in this area; that covers mountains, sea, the town itself of course. Seems most likely, the town doesn't it?'

'Don't ask me! This isn't really my area of expertise. I guess so but perhaps you'd better start with the main man'

Dermot was looking in ore detail at the map, noting the ruins of several houses on the road to Coomnakilla.

'OK, I suppose I'd better go and see the body; not something I'm going to enjoy I suspect. Do you know Jim Kelleher, the pathologist?'

There was a silence that made Dermot glance up from the map to the doctor. McAteer had turned back to the map, 'Oh yes, I know Kelleher well.' Dermot noticed the doctor's look and suspected his professional pride had been hurt by having to hand the case over to the police pathologist. He quickly added.

'Good. I'd like you to work alongside him Andy, since you were there from the start. Is that alright?'

'Thanks Dermot – I'll be on my way.'

After filling in what paperwork he could, the policeman was hurtling towards Killarney up over the twisting mountain roads. He reflected on the problem presented to him. Feeling completely out of his depth he knew that if he didn't find an answer in the next few days detectives from Dublin would be swarming all over the town and he would be dropped from the case. What price the future of the station in Kenmare then? His mission in

Killarney was just as unpleasant as he expected. Kelleher, the pathologist, was already there and was showing McAteer surgical dishes with the lungs, heart, liver and kidneys of the victim. Dermot looked on as the two poked and cut. His feeling that there was no love lost between the two medical men was confirmed by the frosty atmosphere between them. After a few minutes, the pathologist came over to O'Hara and shook hands.

'Good to see you Garda O'Hara. Sad case but interesting from my point of view. The subject's heart was in a dreadful state, so he wasn't long for this world.' Kelleher hesitated, took Dermot by the arm guiding him away from McAteer and towards the window and whispered, 'but it's odd; I can't say for certain that he was murdered. Let's say, experience teaches you to see what's natural and what isn't. I just know there's something wrong here. It's the amount of Lanoxin in his blood...'

'Sorry Jim, what's Lanoxin?'

Kelleher smiled.

'The medical name is Digoxin. It's a drug used to treat cardiac problems, mainly heart failure. In reasonable doses it would keep him alive but he's had a lot more than a reasonable dose. The odd thing is that it's still present. Normally a patient would probably take it first thing in the morning. I would have thought he'd have excreted it – that's one side effect of this particular drug in overdose quantities.' Kelleher, looked into the middle distance as if for inspiration.

'Another peculiar thing - the damage to the kidneys isn't as severe as I would expect. I may have to call his GP in the States to see what he prescribed originally. Anyway, I've sent samples down to the lab for more analysis. I'll call you with the results the moment I have them.'

'Thanks Jim. How long do you think that'll be?'

The pathologist eyed him curiously.

'Someone on your case to get this solved quickly?'

'You're not joking. This guy was a Yank Senator and war hero.'

'Ah. Well whatever his status in life, in death the analysis would be done first thing tomorrow anyway. By the way, his possessions are over there in that bag. Oh yes, you might like to ask your friend Foley about him.'

Dermot shot the pathologist a confused look.

'We found this in his pocket.' Kelleher walked over to a chrome surgical table, rummaged in the polythene bag containing the dead man's possessions and came back carrying a small glossy brochure. He handed it to Dermot. A sentimental picture of a sad eyed seal, flipper raised and with a speech bubble over its head saying, 'Hi!' adorned the front. Across the top was the heading, "Foley's Cruises – the closest you can get to a seal without being a fish!"

'So he must have been on the boat yesterday or the day before.'

'Monday in fact. Foley date stamps these and uses them as tickets.'

'Interesting – thanks for that. See you soon. Right let's go Andy. I have to be in Crowleys around eight. We can jog Peter's memory about our guy.'

Dermot again noticed that McAteer and Kelleher barely exchanged a word as they took their leave.

O'Hara was subdued on the way back but the GP was ebullient. 'Imagine! A fatal poisoning in our little town. And a Yank senator as well. Who says there's no excitement in Kenmare?'

'Too bloody much for me. Anyway Kelleher isn't sure it is poisoning.

'Therefore,' he sighed, 'we're not completely sure it's a murder yet.' muttered Dermot.

'Of course it's poisoning! Clear as a bell – high Digoxin levels in the blood stream. Now who would want to kill him – that's where I have to hand over to you.'

How do you solve a murder that might not be a murder?' 'Listen, thanks for the help today Andy; let me buy you a pint.'

'Now that's the best idea I've heard all day.'

Crowleys Bar 8.20p.m.

As Dermot pushed open the battered front door of Crowley's it was twenty

past eight. He could hear a voice roaring, 'You cannot shoot fish Gordon,

it's immoral and besides the bullet flattens the moment it hits the water so

you've no chance of accuracy. If it worked the Spanish would have machine

guns on every vessel in their fishing fleet!' Foley, standing at the bar, was

addressing his invective to Gordon Loake, a slight, eccentrically dressed, red

haired man seated on a tall stool on his right. To his left a shy man of about

twenty was sipping Guinness and nodding but saying little, overawed by the

eloquence of his companions. Gordon thumped the bar counter and said in a

refined English accent.

'Well I shot a fish in Thailand once just after an encounter with the most

beautiful Thai girl you've ever seen.'

'I've told *you* about that haven't I Denis?'

'You have,' replied the quiet member of the group, 'at least once a week for

about three years.'

'You're all under arrest for talking nonsense,' shouted Dermot above the

noise. Peter Foley wheeled round.

'Are you still in possession of your full authority Garda O'Hara or have you been struck off because we're woefully negligent at creating crime in these parts? So how's the murder going?'

Dermot nearly choked on the pint that had just been handed to him.

'How the hell do you know about that?' Foley looked at the other two and raised his eyebrows. 'We have our sources. Well, the TV to be honest. It was on at six. Standards have slipped. An American Senator can't be quietly murdered these days. At least not in Kenmare.'

'Bloody Norah. There'll be journalists here by morning'

'They're here already,' said Gordon, 'and I told them, for a fee of course, where you were.'

O'Hara glared at Loake.

'You did what? Thanks for making my life hell! I suppose they'll be here any minute?'

'I think not. I informed them you are staying at the Great Southern in Killarney, under an assumed name, to investigate this monstrous crime from there and they all dutifully filed out and left. But I'm afraid I may have let slip Assistant Commissioner Quinn's private phone number.'

Dermot beamed and put his arm round Gordon's shoulder.

'God bless you Gordon you do have your uses sometimes – I apologise for doubting your fluent ability to lie; I will also ignore your extortion of money from innocent journalists and your probable breach of government security regarding Assistant Quinn's number. Gentlemen, you were having an intellectual discussion which I rudely interrupted - please carry on.'

'You can't get off the subject like that Dermot. What did the pathologist say?'

Once again the policeman's mood swung from contentment to irritation. He looked in astonishment at the faces staring his way. 'How come everyone knows so bloody much about this case?'

Denis looked at Dermot sheepishly,

'The sister goes out with someone from the path lab. He.. em... he said they were all very excited to get a look at the insides of a VIP.'

'Really. Well tell him from me he's in contempt of court if he breathes another word. I mean it Denis. Pass that on and make sure he understands. I am so hacked off with this already and the victim is hardly a VIP – he's just an American Senator.'

'OK I'll pass it on. You should have a look at his passport though, it's very impressive'

'What?'

'His passport. He's got stamps in it from all over the world.'

'He's a politician Denis, they travel you know. Where is it now?'

'In his room, 203 – we haven't touched anything – the Boss told me not to until the Gardai, I mean you've, looked at it.'

'Good man, I'll be up first thing in the morning.'

Gordon looked at Dermot in a canny way and then staring straight ahead uttered,

'Of course it may be a complete coincidence but he is, or was, a Shaughnessy.'

'Thank you Gordon for the deep insight. I am only too aware of my lack of experience in solving murders but even a humble Garda can find out a victim's name.'

'Ah well if you won't drink at the fount of wisdom and learn from an acute observer of life I cannot force you.'

Knowing Gordon Loake of old, Dermot felt that perhaps it might be worth his while to listen to the story. Besides he needed some light relief.

'Very well, tell all if you must but at the first suggestion of government conspiracy, aliens or Thai women I will call the discussion to a close.'

Gordon looked round. Not much of a crowd for his great oration. Just his three friends plus Doctor McAteer and the barman, Liam Crowley, who rarely said anything unless it was weather related, or a rather unnecessary,

'Guinness then'?

'All I'm saying is this: Shaughnessy's body was found in remarkably close

proximity to the old house.' He saw that his audience was looking blankly at

him.

'The Shaughnessys? No? Let me give a brief history lesson. Are we sitting

comfortably? No, first we require another round! Six pints please Liam and

you'll have one yourself. The policeman can pay for this one as I'm

informing! Now stay awake at the back, especially you young Denis. The

Shaughnessy house was the site of a particularly nasty bit of land grabbing

in the 1850s. Anthony Shaughnessy had a neighbour called Sean Kelleher.

The two families had lived side by side for probably centuries with no

animosity. However in the heated days of the Great Famine, Kelleher's land

proved to be the more fertile and his family thrived. The Shaughnessys on

the other hand were starving. In those days there was little law about these

parts, you'll forgive me for saying Dermot and the story goes that

Shaughnessy took Kelleher for a little walk one day and in a neighbourly

fashion, pushed him into a bog. The Kelleher family were of course unable

to farm the land without the man of the house but Shaughnessy kindly

offered to help, tilling a bit here, mending a few fences and sowing crops there, eventually taking over all the land and pushing the Kellehers onto a boat bound for the New World. Yet there may be a God or justice somewhere. Because within three years the Shaughnessy household had been reduced to the widow and two boys after a particularly virulent virus swept away five girls, a boy and old Anthony himself, although I say old advisedly; he was only 38 at the time. Life expectancy wasn't much more than that in those days.'

Peter grunted and looked round at the rest of the small audience questioningly.

'Seems hellish unlikely to me! I mean, 150 years after the event you're saying that some local with a grudge has suddenly decided to take revenge.'

Loake put up a hand to silence him. 'Maybe not a local, Peter. The widow Shaughnessy was quite a determined character in her own way. She bundled the kids onto a boat and set off for the States as well.'

Foley was not willing to accept the theory.

'Still seems far fetched. I don't know of any Kellehers apart from some in Bantry and I don't think they're the murdering kind.'

'And our pathologist of course!'

McAteer had been silent up to now but he looked at Dermot as he said this. Dermot laughed.

'What? Do you think Jim Kelleher's drumming up trade by killing people?'

McAteer looked around at the group. He had a serious expression and didn't seem to be joking.

'People round here have long memories and there are some old feuds that will never end. They pass them on from generation to generation like an heirloom.'

Loake interrupted. 'Gentlemen! Kelleher isn't the only suspect we should be looking at.

Dermot stared at him.

'Since when have you been involved in this investigation Gordon?

'Only passing on background information.

'Well just try to stick to that.

'Very well but I have to say that I feel you're barking up the wrong tree, not to say taking a wild stab in the dark and many other metaphors. You Peter are also being far too parochial. When I said not a local, I didn't just mean not from Kenmare. Let me enlighten you with some research I've done today via the modern gossip's equivalent of the corner shop. I refer of course to the internet. Mrs. Shaughnessy, as I said, went to the US. Not only was she a feisty woman but also very attractive. Probably not a patch on the woman I met in Bangkok a few years back. Ah, now she was worth travelling a long way for but sadly....'

'Get on with it Loake or I'll turn you over to the journalists.'

'Very well Dermot. Within six months, she'd met someone and married. His name, you might be interested to know, was McMahon.'

Dermot stopped mid-drink and stared at Loake in disbelief. A smile flitted across his face.

'You're not suggesting?'

He thought back to the night when he'd heard his visitor go out at three in the morning. Loake broke into his thoughts.

'Well, if you were a murderer where would you not be suspected?'

Jumping in before anyone else could answer, he declared.

'In the house of the local policeman or Gardai, as you say over here.'

Dermot stared at him for a few moments, thoughts racing through his head. Turning to Keogh he said, 'Denis, I'd like to see that passport. Let's go.'

Keogh looked shifty, 'Actually we don't need to. I brought it for you.'

Keogh reached inside his jacket and pulled the passport from an inside pocket.

'For God's sake! What are you doing taking evidence from a crime scene? But for now, thanks.'

Flipping it open, he stared at a plethora of destinations.

'Hong Kong, Bangkok, Shanghai four times last year. Paris, Istanbul. London. Shanghai again! Interesting, Look at this. Ho Chi Minh City. I wonder how welcome he was there as a Vietnam veteran! Hmmm when did he leave Bangkok on this trip? Look, he arrived in Bangkok on the 17th October 1998 but there's no exit stamp?'

'The customs wallahs probably didn't bother stamping it.'

Gordon was peering over Dermot's shoulder at the pages.

'When I went to India I wanted my passport stamped and they wouldn't do it. I mean, how can I prove I was there? Bloody bureaucrats! One minute they'll stamp anything that doesn't move but when you want them to they won't. Hopeless.'

'Thanks Gordon for the sermon and the information, that *is* useful. Thanks too for this Denis. I'm off to check if my guest is still about.'

'If there are no more murders tonight I'll see you about ten tomorrow Dermot – don't be late.'

'No, that's fine Peter. By the way, I nearly forgot. Senator Shaughnessy was on your boat last week!'

'Really? Let's have a look at the passport photograph. Oh yeah a white haired American about sixtyish. Of course I remember him.'

'Well? Did he behave oddly?'

'Yeah funny you should say that I'd completely forgotten. He screamed out.
"I'm going to be murdered next week. Help!"

Foley clapped Dermot on the shoulder with a large hand. 'Sorry! I couldn't
help taking the proverbial. My boat is full of white haired, sixty something
Americans every day at this time of year. Ask Martin the mackerel!'

Dermot turned away to leave, annoyed at the fisherman's attitude. As he did
so the door opened, catching him on the right arm. McMahon strode in and
stood in the full glare of five pairs of eyes in the middle of the silent pub.
Denis as ever stared fixedly at the bar. McMahon laughed, breaking the
silence.

'A fine Irish welcome! Let me guess you were talking either about me, my
late compatriot or probably both of us? Am I right?

Loake shrugged, Foley stared straight at the American, trying to read the
other's face for signs of guilt or at least unease and Denis looked at the floor.

'Jo said you'd be here.

'Looking for the bright lights of Kenmare Frank?'

'Maybe something like that. Actually, I wanted to have a word with you
Dermot; on your own. Let me get all you guys a drink first though.'

'OK we'll go through into the back bar.'

McMahon came in through the low door of the bar that was used on rare occasions in summer when the pub was full. Putting a pint down in front of Dermot, he whispered.

'It's this murder.'

'Yes?'

'Well I'm not very good at beating about the bush, so I'll be blunt. You're a small town cop stuck with a big town case. Your bosses are going to have your guts if you don't solve this. They'll close you down and boot you out to some backwater. Am I right?'

'You're certainly right that you don't beat about the bush.' Dermot exhaled deeply. 'And you're about right so far on the career prospects' front. Go on.'

'Well I'll tell you, I was a *great* cop when I was in New York. I loved it. I worked for homicide and I *know* this stuff inside out. We dealt with fifty murder cases a month. I can't say we solved them all but we got a good number of the bastards. Look, I'll be honest. I'm bored. I think I can help in a real big way.'

Dermot looked down at the rickety table with initials gouged into the surface and played with his glass. Looking up he felt his own inadequacy again in sharp contrast with McMahon's confidence.

'OK at the moment I don't feel I have much choice. As you rightly say my bosses are going to close down the station and move me somewhere I don't want to go if this isn't sorted out. So what would be the first thing you'd do?'

McMahon looked at Dermot for a few seconds and weighed his words carefully.

'I'd arrest me and get me down the station as fast as possible for the killing of Senator Mark J. Shaughnessy!'

Dermot slowly put his glass down and stared at McMahon.

'Look at the evidence Dermot – you know I've been tailing this guy around the world. You heard me go out on the night he was killed and yes, I followed him up to the mountain. I'm sure your local sources will have told you about the feud in 1853 and the McMahon family's involvement. I guess that's what the conversation was about just before I came in? What are you waiting for?'

Obligingly McMahon held out his hands.

'What are you doing?' asked O'Hara.

'Put the cuffs on!'

'What? Er, I haven't got any. I'm not sure I've ever seen any here'

His head swimming with the surreal nature of events, he followed McMahon into the main bar. The clatter of conversation stopped and even Gordon's eyes showed a flicker of astonishment as McMahon said,

'You haven't read me my rights yet.'

The others looked round at each other as Dermot said, in a slightly hesitant voice.

'Frank McMahon, I am arresting you for the murder of Senator Mark Shaughnessy Anything you say may be taken down and used against you in evidence at a subsequent trial.'

They walked in silence the three hundred yards to the police station.

'I'm afraid we haven't got a cell ready. My fishing gear's in there.'

'It's OK Dermot. I just wanted you to arrest me in front of the others so word would get out that the killer has been caught and our guy will play his hand more freely. I also wanted to come over here where we definitely wouldn't be overheard.'

'So you didn't kill Shaughnessy?'

'No of course I didn't – although I was tempted to. Yes, I followed him, yes I am a McMahon but that's just an odd coincidence – I'm not related to any McMahons round here - my family only moved to the States in the 1930s. OK, you'd better see this.'

The American pushed an identity card across to Dermot whose head swam even more as he looked at it.

'FBI? You're an FBI agent! What in God's name is going on?'

'Sorry I couldn't tell you earlier. Listen, why don't we head back up to the house I'll give you the background on all this. I must say wherever you guys waste money on this cop shop it's not on heating…'

Dermot got into the car and they drove the three miles to his home.

McMahon sighed and settled himself in the chair that he habitually chose, next to the television in Dermot's front room. O'Hara went out to the kitchen and came back with two glasses. 'A whiskey wouldn't go amiss Frank – now tell me all.'

'Thanks Dermot – to your good health and enlightenment! And an apology for keeping you in the dark about who I am but I had to know I could trust you completely before telling you.'

O'Hara was too intrigued by McMahon's revelation to feel slighted.

'You know I said I was a cop in New York well that was only partly true. After I came back from Vietnam in 73 I got promoted to the plain clothes side and joined the Bureau. It was my Nam experience got me in. I'd worked with military intelligence for a while – it was in Saigon that I met Shaughnessy. We were only kids, he was 23 at the time, but had been made a platoon commander. With all the losses you know, they had to promote even the green behind the ears kind of inexperienced guys. Shaughnessy though was a good guy, very brave, even a bit gung ho. Maybe that had something to do with what happened. In the fight for Quong Tri his platoon got isolated, surrounded, then wiped out. All inside forty minutes. We tried to rescue them, fought off the Cong and I got wounded but he was the only one left alive – just alive I should say. He took seven rounds to his stomach. I don't know what kept him going but they got him back to the States and he recovered, though he left the Army soon after that. I lost contact with him – he travelled for a couple of years then got involved in politics. I knew he was one of the more left wing Democrats who came in with Carter but thought no more of it until one day I was called into my boss's office and handed a dossier and an air ticket. Seems after he left the army he got involved in a support group for ex-vets. Then he started campaigning against the war and became a lot more militant. Understandable you might say but they had some whacky ideas about getting revenge on the US for what had happened to them. His travelling took him to the Soviet Union, Guatemala, Cuba and Libya and that's where we started getting suspicious. His record in the Senate seemed innocent enough but we got concerned after he'd been sitting on a Congressional committee with access to some confidential military material. Nothing too secret, the Pentagon doesn't let Congress into

their big stuff! Anyway, some of this material turned up at a military

briefing in Uzbekistan; this was during Brezhnev's time just after the Soviets

got embroiled in Afghanistan – one of our agents picked it up and eventually

it came full circle back to us. There were three or four possible sources for it

so we fed each of them a different slug of news and waited to see whose

turned up where. Senator Shaughnessy's didn't take long to find its way

into unfriendly hands. In Tbilisi in fact.'

'End of distinguished political career than?'

McMahon shifted on his chair and looked at O'Hara. He was silent for a

moment and O'Hara could see this was an uncomfortable moment for his

guest. Sighing he reflected dispiritedly,

'No, no. Far from it. We couldn't blow his cover without compromising a

major part of our Eastern European network. You know that 'Oh what a

tangled web we weave when first we practice to deceive.' Well it must have

been written about the world of espionage. Our masters wouldn't even let us

confront him with the evidence and question him. I was detailed to track

him and report back on where the information went so we could assess the

potential use it might be put to and the danger to our security.'

'Risky strategy if you ask me,' mused the Garda.

'You're telling me.'

'So how did poor old Kenmare get involved in all this?'

'Dermot this can go no further – is that understood?'

The whiskey and being privy to the secrets of the US government was starting to go to Dermot's head.

'Of course - I understand.'

'Well originally we thought he was meeting Republican groups with Marxist sympathies and the Russians were supporting them in any way they could. In fact we watched your friend Foley – I guess you know he was a bit of a firebrand in his youth?'

Dermot laughed, 'In his youth? He *still* brandishes causes like weapons! You should hear him about the bureaucrats in Brussels. If it had been one of *them* found dead I would have known who was responsible immediately.'

'So, when Shaughnessy went on his boat I thought perhaps there was a drop going on but,' Dermot interrupted.

'No, that's ridiculous! Foley wouldn't get involved in that sort of stuff. He's completely against violence. I think if your traitor wanted to pass on the secrets of catching fish he might have been right but Foley wouldn't engage in anything more, well..' Dermot thought of the word sinister but it didn't seem appropriate in the context of his friend.

'Don't worry, we've cleared Foley you'll be glad to know.'

'I am very glad to hear that. So, what about Shaughnessy? To be honest, unlike you Frank, I don't care about his spying – I just need to know who killed him and why.' He measured his words carefully. 'I mean it *does* seem very convenient from the point of view of your government that he's dead.' McMahon tugged at an earlobe, shrugged and nodded his head slightly. The policeman watched his guest closely.

'I know, I know but rest assured it wasn't us. So who was it you want to know? I think all we have to do is wait, keep our ears and eyes open. In the meantime, how about maybe one more small whiskey then I'm off to bed.' Dermot stretched his legs out gulped back the last of his whiskey and went into the kitchen to refill their glasses. As he looked out of the back window at the distant lights of the town he thought wryly that the American was either a brilliant liar or an innocent FBI man. If there was such a thing.

An oration:

In the small market square people were going about their normal business and a passer by would not have guessed that a major murder investigation was underway. They might however have been drawn to the figure standing on the steps of the bank addressing an audience of journalists and shoppers.

44

'Yes you could say I was instrumental in catching the killer although modesty forbids me from blowing my own trumpet. My extensive research showed that the ancient feud was still alive and well and building towards a deadly dénouement right before our eyes. Deduction, simple really and our police are very grateful to me of course. More's the pity that the authorities didn't involve me in the case a few days earlier. Perhaps this tragedy could have been averted.' Gordon Loake was standing outside the town's main bank conducting an informal press conference with ten journalists and a small group of locals hanging on his every word. One journalist, pushing a microphone at the speaker called out, 'Mr Loake, you *knew* it was the American, Frank McMahon, before the Gardai?' Gordon, beginning to get the feeling of Lincoln at Gettysburg, addressed his admiring audience in an expansive manner.

'Oh yes! The police do a fine job but they don't really have the breadth of experience that a seasoned traveller like myself can bring to bear.' In the crowd Denis watched, and thought, ten seconds to the first mention of his exploits in Thailand. The press might be about to get more revelations than they had bargained for – though it would be doubtful if they could print them. Just as he inwardly counted down to , 'one' he heard the great orator say, 'I remember vividly a young lady called Kamchana in Bangkok….,' there was a commotion and the bystanders looked round. Frank McMahon, had just got out of Dermot O'Hara's car and the two officers of the law strolled across the square towards the bank. They stopped and watched as Gordon's speech ground to a premature halt. 'Carry on Gordon, you were saying,' O'Hara called out, with a broad smile. The waiting journalists' focus switched instantly. Questions were fired at Dermot and his 'prisoner.' 'Mr McMahon, is it true you've been charged with the murder?' one asked. 'I was but I've now been released an innocent man on receipt of further information. That's all I have to say. Now please, can I get through, I really have to get to the bank.' The crowd parted and Dermot and McMahon walked through the group followed by persistent questioning from the media. Gordon had come down from the steps and was waiting for them arms folded and a look of indignation on his face. 'Thank you Garda O'Hara for allowing me to humiliate myself in front of the world's press,' he hissed. 'It could have been worse Gordon. If I hadn't arrived when I did you'd be all over the front page of The Sun tomorrow.'

By the time O'Hara and McMahon left the bank there was no sign of Loake or the press. 'Right, let's go down to the station and work out where we go next.'

As they drove the short distance to the station, Dermot's mind went back to the evening before and he kept thinking about the pathologist. It might be worth checking out his movements over the last 48 hours. Tricky one though. This was a colleague he'd been close to for years, and a well respected forensic practitioner. There was only one way to do this and that was face to face. Explaining the problem to McMahon, he was reassured when the FBI man agreed that discretion was essential.

'Why not invite him out for a beer? That's usually the best way to get information from someone. Get 'em relaxed and question away!'

'Easier said than done. Kelleher's a teetotaller, ' grumbled Dermot. 'Damn, look who's here! That's all I need!'

There, parked outside the police station was a Jaguar, the personal transport of the Assistant Commissioner. As Dermot got out the AC appeared from round the back of the building, rather like an estate agent surveying a juicy prospective sale. 'Well O'Hara, I hear progress has been made? You've arrested an American suspect. Well done.'

O'Hara found it difficult to explain why he'd arrested and released his suspect in quick order. The AC's demeanour changed. 'So what is your next move?'

'I'm going to have a chat with the pathologist.'

'Why? Has he not got the results yet?'

'No. I wish to interview him as a suspect.'

Quinn stared at him.

'Garda O'Hara, I would be very careful if I were you.'

As he explained the background to his reasoning, including Loake's research on an ancient feud, Dermot realised it sounded thin.

The AC stared at his local representative. Breathing in audibly, he looked at O'Hara.

'Let me understand this. You are going to interview an eminent forensic pathologist and accuse him of killing an American Senator because he has the same name as someone who lived two hundred years ago. And all this on the strength of what some drunk in a bar told you?'

At that moment, McMahon moved from where he'd been standing on the steps and looking at the AC said, 'I don't think it's such a bad idea. Where I come from, we rely on local information and knowledge. If there's a chance that someone is involved, no matter how remote they should be interviewed, wouldn't you agree?'

The AC was taken aback by the interruption but something in the American's tone made him listen. Frank looked at him with barely disguised contempt.

'It's a lot more difficult solving crime than deciding how to close down a police station when you're sitting on your ass a hundred miles away!'

With that, he turned and walked into the station leaving the AC and Dermot facing each other. 'I don't know who that is but...

'He's FBI. He's got clearance from our Justice Minister if you'd like to check...?'

The Assistant Commissioner looked perplexed on hearing that the FBI were involved and wondered why he hadn't been told.

'I certainly will check that out for myself. But let me just make it clear if this ends up in the press and you're wrong you carry full responsibility. And I hope your FBI friend discovers his manners.'

With that he got into his car, slammed the door and was driven off. O'Hara smiled as he leapt up the steps.

'You've got some nerve!' he said on reaching the room where Frank was looking at a map on the wall. 'I don't think he'd ever been spoken to like that before.'

'I dare say not. Well, it's good for his soul to hear the truth occasionally. So, our pathologist, let's call him now.' As Dermot reached for the phone it rang.

'Kenmare police station, Garda O' Hara speaking.

Raising his eyebrows he looked at McMahon as if a 20 pound fish had just taken the bait.

'Jim, good to hear from you.' Pointing to McMahon to get him the notepad on the desk opposite, he listened to the pathologist on the other end.

'Really? Listen Jim, could you come over and have a chat about this?' OK if you can't make this afternoon, tomorrow's fine, I understand. Morning would be perfect. Of course.'

McMahon raised an eyebrow as he tried to figure out the other side of the conversation.

'11.30 it is then, all the best Jim, alright.' O'Hara put down the phone and stared at the American. 'Guess what?'

'He has asked to make a full confession and wants a hundred other murders taken into account?'

Dermot bit his lip, passing a hand through his hair and generally giving the impression of a man near the end of his tether.

Frank shook his head. 'It's not good news is it?'

'In all honesty Frank, I don't know. This is like a Rubiks cube or something. You think you're getting near to the solution and suddenly one of the squares is on the wrong side completely.'

'Well, I'm waiting, what's the problem now?'

'Kelleher's certain our man *didn't* die of poisoning.'

'Well, he would say that wouldn't he, if he was the one who did the poisoning.'

Dermot looked at McMahon.

'I believe him. But why if they were up on the mountain together did he not just kill him by strangling or something like that? Poison isn't immediate – especially when it's an overdose of medication that the victim's on anyway. You know nothing about this case makes sense. What would the FBI do?'

'First we'd breathe deeply. Then stop for a moment and review what we've got so far.'

Dermot frowned as he summed up.

'We have a victim who several people, including you, seem to have wanted dead. Our chief suspect at the moment is the pathologist who conducted the autopsy.

'So we ask for a separate autopsy!'

'Like I said I believe him but yes, that would seem a good idea. It's going to be an interesting bit of politics for me to tell our friendly pathologist I want a second opinion...'

Dermot screwed up his face, imagining the interview with the Commissioner if he was wrong.

'Hmmm. Before we go off and create mayhem doing that, I'm going to talk to another contact I have in the path lab. Someone who owes me one.'

O'Hara picked up the phone and dialled.

'Denis, how's it going? Good, glad to hear you're well. Yes. Well I have a bit of bad news. My Commissioner has just heard about your sister's boyfriend leaking information about the pathologist's report. Contempt of court or perverting the course of justice, I think were the words he used. Anyway, if we can prove it, it's an 18 month sentence. Exactly, quite; yes it is a serious position to be in. I don't really know if there is anything I can do for him. Thinking about it though I may be able to help, if you could just get him to the station this afternoon. Oh, about four would be fine. That's grand. Thanks Denis. Yep, see you then.'

Dermot gave McMahon the thumbs up sign. The American grinned and shook his head. 'I'll never trust you again Dermot, you're more devious than some of the hard bitten old guys I used to work with. Let's see what he's got to say.'

At ten to four, a battered Ford Capri pulled up outside the station. Dermot recognized it as Denis Keogh's car. He came up the steps with a pale faced man of about 25 who was shaking. Dermot opened the door and ushered them in. His American came out from the back room.

'This is Paul, Paul McKeever, he goes out with the sister.'

'I'm really sorry Garda O'Hara, I didn't mean to tell anyone about it. I thought Sheila would keep quiet. Honest I'll never do it again.'

McMahon stared at him and showed his FBI id.

'You may never get the chance.' His New York drawl and the id struck a chord of terror with McKeever who was a movie buff and imagined all New York cops were hard mavericks who wouldn't think twice about 'wasting,' a suspect. Dermot played the good cop.

'Well hopefully we won't have too many murders where you'll have the chance. It was a stupid thing to do. But you just might be able to get yourself off the hook if you can tell me a few things. I'll hand you over to my American colleague here.'

Paul flinched and stared at the American. He noticed McMahon's scars and felt he could expect no mercy. O'Hara looked up, 'Thanks Denis, you can go now.'

McKeever's fear levels rocketed as he realised he'd be on his own.

'You're sure you don't want me to stay and give him moral support?

'I'm not sure how moral your support might be – on you go.'

'See you Paul,' Denis muttered, and shambled out, looking as thought he'd taken his leave of a condemned man, minutes before the scaffold loomed.

The door closed and they heard him drive off.

'OK , I want to know what you guys in the path lab found in Shaughnessy's body?'

'What, what about the contempt of court thing?' he stammered.

'That can wait. You tell me all you can.

Whatever anyone said about this lad's naivety he was smart when it came to his job. After forty minutes Dermot had a good picture of how the drug worked and why it couldn't have killed Senator Mark Shaughnessy.

'So you're telling me that the drug was administered after this guy was dead?

'That's right. The first indication was that the amount in the body was still too concentrated in the blood. Of course, after death there is no blood flow so the drug couldn't be distributed throughout the body.'

'So, are you saying someone found his body up at Coomnakilla and injected it with Digoxin?'

'No, it was done later than that.'

'Later? When?'

'Either while it was in the path lab or on the way there. But I'm sure it was in the lab.'

McMahon butted in.

'And what makes you so sure of that? Don't tell me you can tell to the second when the stuff was injected?'

McKeever looked down and then back up at the two men in front of him as he struggled with the words.

'No, I. You see, I saw him doing it.'

Dermot looked at McMahon and they interrupted each other with the same question.

'Who? Who was it?'

Paul looked terrified.

'I'd just gone into the sterile area at the back of the lab. The pathologist hadn't arrived – he'd been delayed in town. The mountain rescue guys brought him in, the body that is. I heard them leave and thought I'd better start preparing the instruments. I looked through into the lab and in the mirror I saw Dr McAteer injecting the body.'

'McAteer? You'd better be very sure of your ground here. If you're lying, I'll make sure you get the maximum sentence. Didn't you say anything?'

Knowing how shy Paul was, he knew the answer before McKeever said,

'I pretended I hadn't seen anything - I didn't know if it was something he should do or not but I didn't know what to say.'

McMahon jumped in.' Did you tell Kelleher?'

'No, I wasn't sure what I'd seen really, until this morning.'

'Why this morning?'

'I found this.' The path lab assistant took a syringe wrapped in plastic, from his pocket. 'Just after Dr McAteer injected the body, Mr Kelleher walked in and I heard Dr McAteer push something under a cupboard. He called today to ask if anything had been found in the path lab and I said no the cleaners had been in. He sounded relieved.'

'Is that all he said?'

'He told me he thought he'd dropped a medical instrument and if it turned up to call him.'

Instinct told Dermot that McKeever wasn't lying. Yet why his friend should have done such a bizarre thing, he couldn't fathom.

'Can I go now?'

Dermot looked up. He'd forgotten anyone else was present. Sighing he thought it over briefly. 'Have you any other questions Agent McMahon?'

Frank, looking surprised at being addressed in this way, shook his head.

'For the moment, no. Don't go too far though, we may want to talk to you again. And thanks Paul, you've been a great help.

'What about the contempt charge? Can you do anything about that? What contempt charge? Oh, yes. I'll have a word.'

'Thanks Garda O'Hara, I'd better go and tell Sheila.'

'Just make sure you do not breathe a word of what we've discussed to anyone! Not even Sheila. Do you understand?'

McKeever nodded, sprinted for the door and was gone.

'What do you make of that?' Dermot asked McMahon.

'Quite a surprise to say the least. Is there any reason why McAteer should want to make it look as though Shaughnessy was poisoned? What if he wanted to make people think Kelleher had killed him?'

'I can't think of any reason for that. But.'

The American could see O'Hara was worried.

'But what?'

'Well, I just remember when I told McAteer that Kelleher was doing the autopsy he looked... at the time I thought it was just his professional pride or curiosity or something.'

'Can you speak a little less like the oracle of Delphi and a bit more like a cop Dermot!

'Sorry, Frank. Andy McAteer looked really angry when I told him that. He's such an easy going character normally but there was real hatred in his eyes, now I think about it. At the time, I thought I was being a bit paranoid.

And just forgot about it. But with this. The problem is of course he's a friend a well.'

'OK do you know of any connection between them. I mean are they related? Have they ever shared a practice? There are all sorts of connections and professional rivalries doctors can have.'

'Not that I know of – I wonder if Loake or Foley have any ideas on this. Listen, we'll see them in Crowleys this evening. Don't mention what we've just heard. Let's hear what they have to say.

On weekdays Crowley's had a small but loyal clientele consisting of Denis, Gordon, Peter and frequently Dermot. The doctor would often drop in as well and Dermot was relieved to see he wasn't there when he and Frank pushed open the door shortly after 9. From the bar three pairs of eyes stared at them as they came in.

'Loake's been telling us you disrupted his speech to the good people of Kenmare this morning Dermot,' said Peter loudly as he saw his friend, 'shame on you, just as he was getting to the ripe material as well.'

Dermot grunted and Foley could see he was worried. 'Let me get you a drink – and what would you like Frank?'

'Any chance of a cocktail? Maybe a Sidecar?' he asked hopefully.

The barman looked up at McMahon from the racing pages and stared at him for a second as if the American had asked to sleep with his sister.

'Y'could try a Guinness and lager.' he offered tentatively.

'No, I'll stick with what you do best.'

O'Hara looked at Keogh, 'Denis, your friend McKeever went free, a scared but innocent man. Thanks for getting him over to me – very useful.'

Loake was looking from one to the other, irritated that something had been going on without his knowledge. Coughing softly, apparently addressing the air he said,

'I assume things are moving behind the scenes, mysterious forces of the Gods propelling us mere mortals helplessly and inexorably towards the dénouement as we sit here. Unwitting pawns in this grand drama?'

'Something like that, but I hope you're not too unwitting tonight. I need information. Maybe from you as well, Peter.'

Loake and Foley exchanged a surprised glance.

'You want us to turn supergrass?' queried Loake.

'Not quite. I just need to know how well you think Kelleher and McAteer get on? I mean, I know they know each other professionally but apart from that?'

Loake looked at the floor. 'Well I don't know the man in Killarney but of course I know McAteer and he seems, reserved, shall we say, in his admiration for Kelleher. Just from what I've heard him say.'

Peter looked at them all. 'I take it you have a good reason for asking this?'

Dermot sighed.

'That's the problem I've got a reason but it doesn't make sense.'

'Well to start with I can tell you that they both studied medicine at UCD together.'

'Surely Kelleher is quite a bit older than McAteer?'

'Aye, apparently he'd already done a degree in chemistry before he switched to medicine. He was a mature student when they met up.'

Foley went silent. Dermot took a sip. Looking at Peter he could tell the big fisherman was reluctant to continue.

'Go on. They were at UCD together. And…'

'I think this would be better conducted in private,' he said glancing around his companions.

'No! I protest,' said Loake, slamming his glass on the bar, worried that tidings of great moment were about to escape him yet again.

O'Hara looked round at the group.

'Right Peter let's go. Is the back room open Liam?'

'Yeah, go on ahead there. I'll just give the fire a bit of a stoke for you.'

Dermot led the way with Peter following.

'This seems to be becoming the command centre,' he joked as they watched Liam work his magic with the poker, turning a few embers into a blazing fire. He went out, closing the door behind him.

The policeman looked at the roaring fire for a second then at the face of his companion.

'I suppose it's only fair to tell you what's going on.'

'Might be useful. Then I can give you a bit more background on the doc.'

Dermot gave a quick run down of what he'd been told of the events in the path lab. Foley whistled and pulled his beard.

'Bloody idiot, what did he do that for?'

'That's what I want to know.'

After a huge sigh Foley said, 'Actually I think I know. I feel I'm betraying him Dermot but you'd better know this.'

'McAteer and Kelleher were at college together. They became good friends and stayed that way until McAteer fell in love with Kelleher's wife.'

'What? How did he meet her?'

'Like I told you. They were good friends, Kelleher invited McAteer to his house, he became a frequent visitor and that's where he met the former Mrs Kelleher.

'Former?'

'They're divorced now. Because of McAteer. He stayed with her for about six months after she left Jim, then ran off with some other woman.'

'My God, I wouldn't have put our doctor down for a Casanova. The quiet ones and all that. Strange they should end up in the same neck of the woods.'

'Hmm. I wonder if it was an accident?'

'In what way?'

'Kelleher got McAteer chucked out of medicine, it must have seemed like the end of his career.'

'How?'

'He showed the college authorities evidence that McAteer had been stealing drugs from the pharmacy.

Dermot thought for a second about what Foley was telling him.

'Not a good start for a medical student. So how come he's a doctor now. Oh no. Do you think he's practising but not qualified?

Foley shook his head.

'No, you're letting the excitement of this investigation get to you. He went over to England and qualified there – I think the college authorities knew there was more to this than met the eye but couldn't work out what it was so they didn't put it on his record. 'Unorthodox to say the least,' muttered Frank

'Maybe but at least they had some sense of justice'

McMahon was unable to contain himself.

'And had he been?'

'What?

'Stealing drugs?

'No, not at all. I believe someone else stole the drugs, in fact I'm sure. Someone you know very well Dermot.'

Peter motioned the two policemen closer. Foley's, McMahon's and O'Hara's heads were nearly touching. The fisherman whispered one word. Dermot, knocked over his pint which landed in McMahon's lap. The American barely noticed he was so dazed by what he'd heard. A number of expletives followed. In the front bar, Loake looked at Denis and Liam.

'Well, as always it looks like we're going to be the last to know. I suppose another drink might while away the dull moments until our enlightenment. Liam!'

Early next morning as he and Frank drove along the coast road, Dermot marvelled again at the beauty of the place. Foley had once asked him, 'Why in God's name do all these people from places like New York and Tokyo decide to come here? I mean do they wake up one morning with a burning desire to visit Kenmare? Weird, if you ask me.'

Conversely, Dermot could not see why anyone would want to live anywhere else. It had fishing, Crowley's pub, stunning surroundings and well, more fishing; point proven. As he watched a large coaster slowly making its way westward he began to rehearse what he was going to say to Jim Kelleher. 'Jim I hear you tried to set McAteer up with drugs when you were at university?' A bit blunt perhaps. This was going to be a lot trickier than it had first appeared. What if Foley had got the story wrong? As he approached the station where he'd arranged to meet the pathologist he saw a familiar car parked at the front.

'What does *he* want?

'Good morning Garda O'Hara!'

'Good morning Assistant Commissioner Quinn.'

'I assume the investigation is going well?'

'Very well. I just have to check out a few things with Jim Kelleher and then I should have something to tell you.'

'Well I hope so, this seems to be dragging on a bit.'

The Commissioner watched as Kelleher drove up.

'Morning Jim, are you well?'

'Very well indeed thanks Martin.'

In all the years Dermot had known the Commissioner, he had never heard anyone call him by his first name. In fact he wasn't even sure he'd known that the Commissioner's first name was Martin. In a moment of irreverence, he thought of Foley's Martin the mackerel. The Commissioner called Dermot over to the car. 'O'Hara, be careful how you treat Mr. Kelleher. I don't want to hear any complaints from him. What's your Yank chum doing here?'

'Well since he was investigating Shaughnessy, it's only right that he's involved with my line of inquiry.'

'When you've completed your 'chat' with Jim, I'd like to have a word about the future of this station. I'll be here in my car.'

Dermot smiled, 'Of course, I can make time for that Mr. Quinn.'

Frank had gone ahead into the police station and was scribbling on a note pad, as Dermot and the pathologist entered the echoing front room that could have accommodated an entire squad of policemen.

'You don't mind if I sit in on this do you?'

The FBI man asked the pathologist, in a tone that didn't expect 'no' for an answer.

'Not at all. Now, how can I help you Dermot?'

Dermot stopped for a moment. He got up and stared into the distance. He could see the mountain where this whole business had started.

'How well do you know Assistant Commissioner Quinn?'

'We were at university together. He's been a friend of mine since then.'

'Really? Now that's interesting. All roads seem to be leading back to Dublin.'

'What do you mean?

'You were at UCD with Dr. McAteer as well, weren't you?

Kelleher's face darkened and he looked out of the window as if gathering his composure. 'Yes, he was there for a while when I first went to UCD. That was a long time ago now.'

'How did you get on with him?'

'Fine. What's this got to do with the post mortem I carried out on the American?

'It has everything to do with it. You fell out with McAteer didn't you?'

'You've done your research well Dermot. Yes. And I'm sure you know why. He behaved dishonourably.'

'Did you set him up – plant drugs on him to destroy his career?'

'How the hell? Kelleher stopped but he knew there was no point lying. Silence filled the room as Kelleher struggled with the guilt he'd felt all these years.

McMahon butted in.

'It's a straightforward question Mr. Kelleher, did you or did you not get McAteer thrown off his course by planting drugs in his room.'

'It wasn't my idea. It didn't happen like that. It was stupid, I agreed to it because…'

Frank McMahon, stood up from the side table and came over.

'Because what Mr. Kelleher? Because someone offered to do it for you.'

McMahon paused before asking the next question.

'What was Mr Quinn doing at this university?'

'Psychology.'

'And what was he doing outside study hours?'

'I don't know.'

'Really? That's very odd. Your other classmates all knew – they called him 'Plod' didn't they? That was his nickname?'

'Yes, I think it was something like that.'

'He was on secondment wasn't he? In the police force and studying for a degree - very admirable. What wasn't so admirable was his theft of drugs.'

Dermot didn't know if he or Kelleher had turned more pale.

'While you were in town yesterday I took the liberty of asking one of my colleagues to check up on Mr Quinn's career. Guess where he started out?'

O'Hara didn't even have to think for a moment. 'Drug Squad by any chance?'

'Got it in one Dermot. He was a very brilliant cadet and after training Quinn was immediately sent to Dublin where, I believe, they had a huge drugs problem. So Kelleher has a heart to heart with his buddy Quinn who was studying psychology on secondment from Narcotics or as you say the Drug Squad. Quinn knows his stuff and 'borrows' a controlled drug Diamorphine, because it has to be one that the medical faculty will have as well and that McAteer could plausibly get his hands on. Am I about right so far?'

Kelleher looked at him like a rabbit in the headlights and nodded.

McMahon continued, 'They were all friends in the hall of residence, in and out of each others' rooms all the time. It was easy for Quinn to plant the drug in McAteer's room.' McMahon turned and glared at Kelleher. 'Then with his other hat on he alerted his narcotics pals to raid the residence. McAteer got caught. Simple. But strangely Quinn did not arrest him and push for a prosecution, saying there was enough doubt about the case for it not to go to criminal prosecution. Of course the college authorities aren't as demanding as a jury and any hint of drug problems for a medical student means the end of their course and possibly career. Dermot looked at Kelleher.

'What in God's name were you thinking? And what did Assistant Commissioner Quinn think he was doing?'

Kelleher sat with his head in his hands. Then looking up at Dermot, he said. 'McAteer had destroyed my life. I discovered he was having an affair with Claire, my wife. We'd only been married a few months. I was so in love with her. I was stupid but he was despicable! I'd invited him into my home and we'd befriended him but he betrayed us, me.' O'Hara frowned and looked from his American colleague to the pathologist.

'What I don't understand is this. Why get Quinn involved and why did he behave in such a reckless way? Risky business for a friend wasn't it? Seems to have over-reacted a bit?'

Kelleher frowned and looked at Dermot.

'Claire, my ex-wife, is Quinn's sister. I told Quinn about her and McAteer and he went ballistic. He said I couldn't let McAteer get away with it – I think he even said that honour had to be satisfied! As you probably know Dermot, he's a bit of a puritan. Our other nickname for him, which even the FBI don't seem to have picked up on, was "Cromwell". He said if I really wanted revenge, he could do it. I just agreed without thinking. Then after all those years McAteer turns up one day. He'd trained in England and eventually he came back to practice in Ireland. I guess I'd better get a lawyer to represent me?'

McMahon looked at Kelleher with some sympathy. Dermot was tapping the table as he went through the story once more.

'Frank, would you ask Assistant Commissioner Quinn to come in and join us?

The Assistant Commissioner did not look pleased as he strode up the steps and entered the room.

'O'Hara, I asked you to come out to my car to talk about the future of this station.'

'We are going to talk about the future of this station Assistant Commissioner, but first we're going to look at a case of perverting the course of justice.'

Quinn looked at him askance then at Kelleher, who was pale and trembling.

'Martin, I had to tell them, they knew anyway.'

'Tell them what Jim?'

'About the,' he paused struggling to find the words, 'the incident with Andy McAteer at UCD.'

Quinn folded his arms, sat back and a faint smile flitted across his face.

'What incident would that be?'

McMahon but with a voice that masked a threat said quietly, 'Stealing drugs from a secure police site, planting drugs on a fellow student and using police resources to make a false arrest.'

'And you're going to prove this I suppose?' sneered Quinn.

The American stood and for a moment Dermot thought he was going to attack his superior. He wasn't quite sure where his loyalties lay but McMahon just said in a cold voice.

'There's something I haven't shown you yet Quinn.'

'Assistant Commissioner to you!' Quinn's voice rose and he glared at the American.

'For the moment of course you are Assistant Commissioner Quinn,' McMahon remarked casually as he reached into an inside pocket and pulled out his FBI id. 'I have a lot of resources to draw on, and their research, which will stand up in court, is watertight. I have been liaising closely with your Minister for Justice who wants me to keep him up to date with our progress. By a stroke of luck he's down here at his holiday home. If you could pass me the phone Dermot.'

He dialled a number and sat back. 'Good afternoon Minister it's Frank McMahon here. That's right. I'm fine thank you. Good. Listen I've got Assistant Commissioner Quinn and Jim Kelleher here with me. Yes, Garda O'Hara has been an immense help to me and I'd like to meet up so I can update you on our progress. Yes I can be at the hotel in thirty minutes. I know where it is. I'll be in the lobby'

The other three in the room looked at McMahon. If the American could summon a government minister just like that, he certainly had some clout. Dermot beckoned to McMahon. They went out to the corridor, shutting the door behind them.

'Well?' queried McMahon. Dermot looked at him. 'I've got an idea.' He checked the door and whispered to McMahon who smiled, then laughed aloud. 'Dermot, you are a devious so and so. Are you quite sure you weren't involved in all this?' Opening the door they entered to a sepulchral silence. Sunlight streamed in and naturally, Dermot's thoughts turned to fishing. A fine evening like this would be perfect for a spot of fly fishing on the local river...

Quinn shifted uneasily as they came back in. He felt out of control and thought as fast as he could.

'Garda O'Hara, Mr. McMahon,' he spoke in a measured way, 'we all, as young men, do, well, foolish things at times.' Looking at McMahon he smiled ruefully, 'but usually the FBI isn't at hand to expose our folly. I know what Jim and I did was wrong. It was a hot headed response to a terrible act of betrayal.'

'Mr Quinn, the pair of you perverted the course of justice and could have destroyed McAteer's career and put him in jail.'

'And what do you think McAteer's just tried to do to me?' asked Kelleher.

'I know.

O'Hara paused. He was enjoying himself and didn't want to rush the moment.

'That's why I've come up with a solution.'

Quinn and Kelleher exchanged worried glances.

Dermot looked out the window.

'Here's Andy now.'

As the doctor walked into the room and saw his two former friends his face fell.

'I can imagine what this is about Dermot. I know, I know. I will make a full statement. I believe there are mitigating circumstances but I was an absolute idiot to do what I did.'

McMahon spoke.

'So join the idiots' club. There seem to be a lot in this room!'

Dermot pulled over a chair from the side room, 'Sit down there Andy. I think we need to look at this situation carefully. As far as I can see all three of you have committed criminal offences for much the same reasons - to avenge a slight, whether real or perceived doesn't matter much. If the law runs its full course all three of you are heading for jail and the destruction of your reputations. Now I'm not interested in revenge for anything and nor, as far as I know, is Frank here. What I am interested in is keeping this police station open. Looking over at the Assistant Commissioner O'Hara could see an expression of, was it admiration or perhaps relief on his senior officer's face?

'I know Assistant Commissioner that might be a problem for you but I'm also aware that Dr. McAteer has been given three months notice on his surgery premises.

McAteer nodded in a resigned way.

Quinn again looked puzzled.

Dermot continued, 'What I'm saying is that I will close this case. After all, we know the poor old Senator, who seems to have been forgotten in all this, wasn't murdered. But the deal is that you, Assistant Commissioner, will argue the case for this building to stay open as a combined police station and surgery.'

Raising an eyebrow at O'Hara and taking a deep breath, Quinn looked at the others.

'I can't see why that wouldn't work, emphasising the benefit to the community and so on. If that would work for you Dr. McAteer, I'm sure the Gardai would be happy to lease the spare room to you as your surgery. Garda O'Hara, I must commend you on your political as well as detective skills. I seem to remember you saying that you used that room for your meetings with local people? We wouldn't want to inconvenience you on that score.'

Dermot thought of all his fishing tackle in the upstairs room.

'There's an equipment room I've been meaning to clear out – I can use that.'

Crowley's Bar: 8.45

McMahon, Dermot and Joanne arrived at Crowleys to find a small but expectant crowd already there. McMahon pushed his way through the group at the bar. Loake, turned and looked Dermot up and down.

'You look extremely pleased with yourself Garda O'Hara. Are you going to give us mere mortals an inkling as to what great news you have to impart?'

'I am,' said Dermot as he motioned for drinks for Joanne, McMahon and himself.

'You can overdo the dénouement you know,' answered Loake.

'I have solved one of the thorniest problems I've ever met.'

'You got the killer!' Denis' admiration was clear to see as he stared at the policeman.

'No, I've managed to find someone to rent half the police station so I'm not going to end up in some God-forsaken town a million miles from the sea.'

Loake beamed.

'Now that's what I call a result. Slainte!'

Dermot held up his hand. When the bar was silent, he waited a moment, enjoying the drama.

'And I have solved what I will call, the incident of the American Senator.'

'I knew you would, said Loake, I never doubted your detective skills for a moment.'

'I will ignore that blatant perjury and just say that I was helped hugely by Frank and Peter in getting to the centre of this very peculiar maze.'

Loake coughed quietly and looked at O'Hara.

'Oh, of course, Gordon. I have to acknowledge *your* contribution.'

Denis could contain himself no longer.

'So who was the murderer Garda O'Hara?

Dermot took a drink;

'There was no murder and therefore no murderer.'

'No!'

The disappointment in Denis's voice and Loake's face made Dermot smile. He spread his arms in an expansive gesture.

'However, Assistant Commissioner Quinn has generously agreed not to close our police station and indeed to help his old friend Andy McAteer by leasing part to him for his surgery.'

'Well, that's not a bad day's haul Dermot,' said Peter Foley. 'I think I know how you did it but the word blackmail will not pass my lips. Again.'

'There are wheels within wheels here and I call it a deeply unsatisfying resolution to the whole thing', said Loake, scowling at Liam who carried on reading the evening paper.

Dermot shrugged, 'Isn't it better that we can sleep safe in our beds knowing there is no homicidal maniac stalking the streets of our town?'

Loake looked at him, 'No! Well, yes, in a way but...'

'So. Do any of you know what happened?'

They all turned to look in astonishment. The question had come from behind the bar. To their certain knowledge, this was the first time Liam Crowley had spontaneously ventured a question apart from, 'Guinness then?'

'Well Liam', O'Hara started, 'this was, if you like, an ordinary death pretending to be a murder.'

'No, not about that. What won the three thirty at Leopardstown? The result's not in the paper.'

The combined might of the FBI, Gardai and local intelligence services stood around helpless. Liam stared at them briefly then sighed in disappointment.

'Ah well. I'll phone the mother, she'll know. Guinness then?'

THE END

Did you enjoy Thicker Than Water?

If you enjoyed meeting the characters in 'Thicker Than Water', you will love 'Banshee', the full length, gripping follow up in the Dermot O'Hara series. It is available on Amazon at the following link.

http://tinyurl.com/bansheer2

Turn the page for a taste of

Chapter One

Storm was coming to Kenmare. Even before the wind sang a keening dirge through the rigging of his fishing boat, the 'Saoirse', Peter Foley sensed the birth of the gale in the late January afternoon. A less experienced fisherman might not have noticed the hint of a ripple across the sullen, steely water and a slight change in the direction of the wind. But Foley had fished and navigated the waters round Kenmare for more than twenty years and knew the moods of sea and weather better than he knew himself. It was no surprise to him when a harsh squall blew down the glen whipping hail like shrapnel across the lough and the bow of his fishing boat. Foley steered the 'Saoirse' back towards the distant town where through the dusk he saw the lights coming up in the windows of shops on the harbour front. From out on the water he could hear rigging slapping against masts as the wind picked up and knew that steep seas would soon chop and churn across the inlet, making any attempt to enter the harbour hazardous. Suddenly his radio crackled and the coastguard, Tom Hartigan, an old friend of Foley's, interrupted his concentration.

'Kenmare Coastguard to Saoirse, Kenmare Coastguard to Saoirse, can you hear me Saoirse?'

'Saoirse to coastguard of course I can bloody hear you! How's it going Tom?'

'Hiya Peter. Listen, we're getting reports of a storm reaching force nine or ten out beyond Blasket. Where are you at the minute?

'Nowhere near there Tom – I'll be home in ten minutes or so.'

The coastguard was about to break communication with the Saoirse and turn his attention to another fishing boat when he heard Foley exclaim,

'Bloody hell!'

'Peter? What is it?'

'Hold on a moment will you?'

There was a long pause but Tom could still hear Foley on the bridge of the Saoirse and the shrill sound of his fish detection sonar in the background.

'I've got a sonar reading – there's something huge right below us. It's massive! Look at that!

'Are you close to shore?'

Foley peered out into the gathering squall.

'No I'm right in the middle of the channel; off Coss Strand. It's not like a shoal, more like, well, one object. This is showing… hold on it's moving back under me. Wow! Look at the speed of that. Gone – just like that! I'm going to turn and see if I can pick it up.'

'Saoirse I wouldn't advise that – this storm's closing in very quickly. We're requesting all vessels return to port. Do you hear me?'

Foley put down the transmitter and swung the Saoirse's bow out towards the open sea again. His fisherman's instinct was excited by the idea of a basking shark or maybe even a whale somewhere out there in the darkness. Dusk and rain had closed in completely and looking over his shoulder he could barely see the lights of the town through the gloom. His sonar now showed no trace of anything moving, so reluctantly he turned the helm and nudged the vessel across the roughening, white capped waters back towards shelter. Just as she was broadside to the tide a wave, bigger than anything he had ever seen in the bay, rose and bore down on the boat. Foley pushed the throttle forward, gunned the engine and at the same time swung the helm as fast and hard as he could but the wave picked the Saoirse up and rolled her over on to her port side before lifting her high on its crest. Peter braced his huge frame against the side of the wheel-house gripping on to the wheel to try to keep control but all he could see around him through the wheelhouse windows was foaming water. The last thing he heard was the radio bursting into life as water smashed through the starboard window filling the wheelhouse, turning it into a maelstrom of broken glass and wood.

'Kenmare coastguard to Saoirse, Kenmare coastguard to Saoirse. Come in Saoirse!'

There was silence. Tom Hartigan glanced across the room to his colleague Shane McDonnell and hit the transmit button again.

'Kenmare coastguard to lifeboat we need your assistance. We may have a capsize; last reported position mid channel between Coss Strand and Dromore. Vessel is the Saoirse out of Kenmare. Forty foot fishing boat skippered by Peter Foley.'

Even as he was speaking to the lifeboat captain Conor Fitzpatrick, Hartigan heard a maroon go off calling the crew to action stations. Peering out through the worsening gale hammering sheets of rain against the windows, Hartigan felt immense admiration for the courage of the volunteers who manned the lifeboat in every season and under all conditions. Fitzpatrick asked, 'You're sure it's Peter Foley's boat?'

'That's correct Con.'

There was a short silence

'My God, he'll need all his experience in this weather. That's dreadful news Tom.'

He switched back to professional mode.

'Was anyone else on board with him?

'No, I saw him going out. He was on his own.'

'OK the crew's here. I'll be in contact after we launch.'

'Thanks Con - take care and keep the channel open; let me know if you find anything.'

'Will do. See you later.'

From Hartigan's vantage point looking down at the harbour he had seen one car arrive and another crew member sprint from a shop to the lifeboat station. That would be Tony Geraghty, a close personal friend of Peter Foley. The 'Eleanor Moody' was now moving down the slipway and she launched straight into the teeth of the storm, a huge plume of spray shrouding her bow. Hartigan watched the lifeboat safely clear the harbour, sighed and turned to his second in command.

'Shane, will you call Dermot O'Hara. Break it to him gently but tell him we may have lost the Saoirse – ask him to get down here as quick as he can. I'll get Dr. McAteer and the ambulance.'

~ ~ ~

To start reading the rest of 'Banshee' in under a minute click here on one of the following links

'Banshee' on Amazon.com

'Banshee' on Amazon.co.uk

Reviews of '*Banshee*'
"Truly fantastic read!
Simply outstanding literature. There is a fair sense of humour, drama, and unlike any other book I have read, I felt truly empathetic towards the characters in the novel. If you are reading this very brief review, please read this book!"

"A Great Read!
I nearly didn't write this review because I couldn't think of a title that differed from two other reviewers! The characterisation and the vivid description of the South West of Ireland captured this reader's attention immediately. This quality of writing, combined with a terrific plot, draws you in to the point that you are no longer reading the book, but are observing the story unfold from a corner of Crowley's bar! This is a superb read and I'm looking forward to the next offering from this author."

CPSIA information can be obtained
at www.ICGtesting.com
Printed in the USA
LVOW08s1454030817

543710LV00031B/799/P